Mighty

SPACE ROBOTS

THOMAS KINGSLEY TROUPE

Bolt is published by Black Rabbit Books
P.O. Box 3263, Mankato, Minnesota, 56002.
www.blackrabbitbooks.com

Marysa Storm, editor; Grant Gould, interior designer; Michael Sellner, cover designer; Omay Ayres, photo researcher

Library of Congress Cataloging-in-Publication Data
Names: Troupe, Thomas Kingsley.
Title: Space robots / by Thomas Kingsley Troupe.
Description: Mankato, Minnesota : Black Rabbit Books, [2018] | Series: Bolt. Mighty bots | Audience: Age 9-12. | Audience: Grade 4 to 6. | Includes bibliographical references and index.
Identifiers: LCCN 2016049963 (print) | LCCN 2016050299 (ebook) | ISBN 9781680721607 (library binding) | ISBN 9781680722246 (e-book) | ISBN 9781680724639 (paperback)
Subjects: LCSH: Space robotics–Juvenile literature. | Robotics–Juvenile literature.
Classification: LCC TL1097 .T76 2018 (print) | LCC TL1097 (ebook) | DDC 629.8/920919-dc23
LC record available at https://lccn.loc.gov/2016049963

Printed in the United States at CG Book Printers, North Mankato, Minnesota, 56003. 8/18

Image Credits

Alamy: dpa picture alliance, 16–17; Science Photo Library, 22 (top); apod.nasa.gov: NASA, 12; Commons.wikipedia.org: Rept0n1x, 7; Dreamstime: Konstantin Kowarsch, 8–9 (rover); mars.nasa.gov: NASA, 15; Science Source: David Ducros, 8 (robotic arms); NASA, 4–5; NASA/JPL, 9 (probe); Shutterstock: 300ad, 3, 28–29, 32; Andrea Danti, 24–25; Andrey Armyagov, Cover, 8 (satellite), iurii, 6, Back Cover; Marc Ward, 1; Nerthuz, 31; www.nasa.gov: the Hubble Heritage Team, 9 (background); NASA, 11, 22 (bottom), 27; NASA/Dmitri Gerondidakis, 18–19; NASA/JPL-Caltech/Stanford, 21

CONTENTS

CHAPTER 1

ROBOTS in Space

Millions of miles from Earth, six wheels roll across red dust. A robot explores the planet Mars. It stops to take pictures. Then it uses a little scoop to collect soil. The robot's name is Curiosity. It's exploring where no humans have gone before.

Exploring the Unknown

Most robots are built to make life easier on Earth. But some are made to travel into the unknown. They are built to explore space. These bots help humans learn about places far, far away.

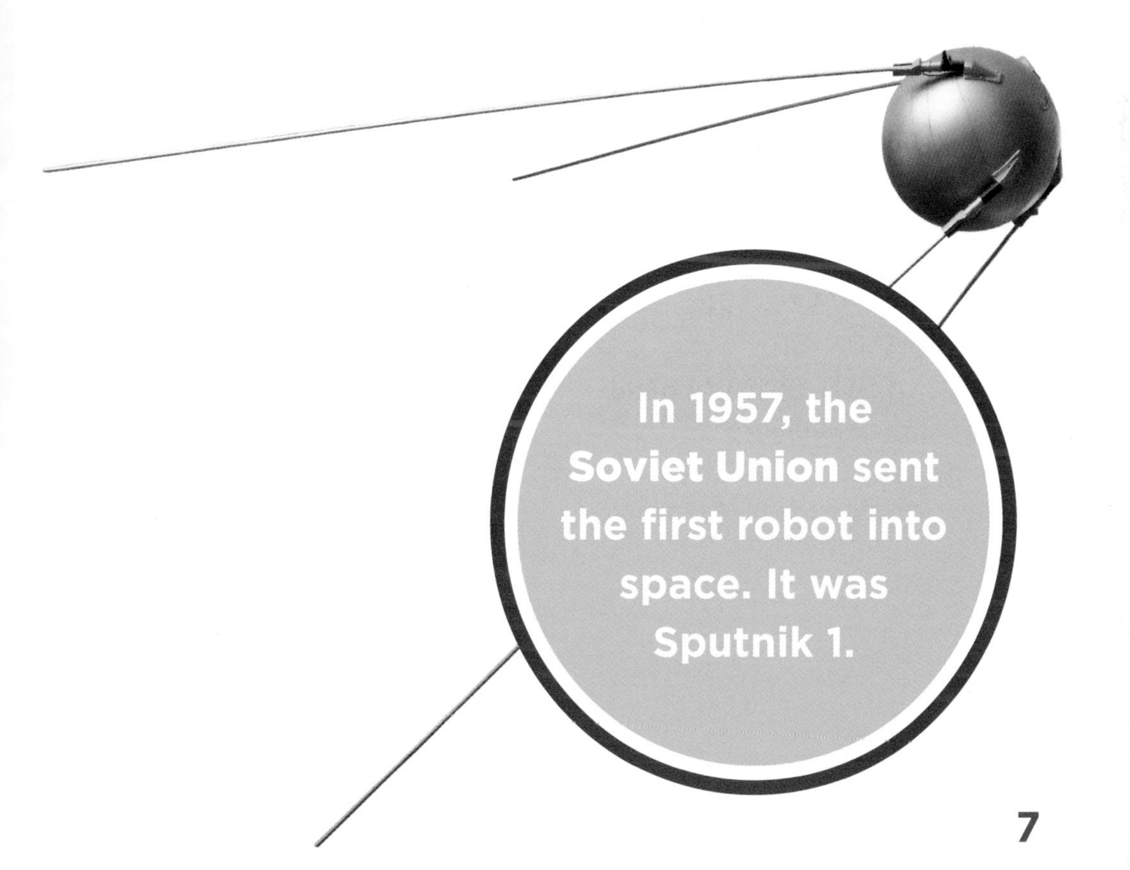

In 1957, the Soviet Union sent the first robot into space. It was Sputnik 1.

TYPES OF SPACE ROBOTS

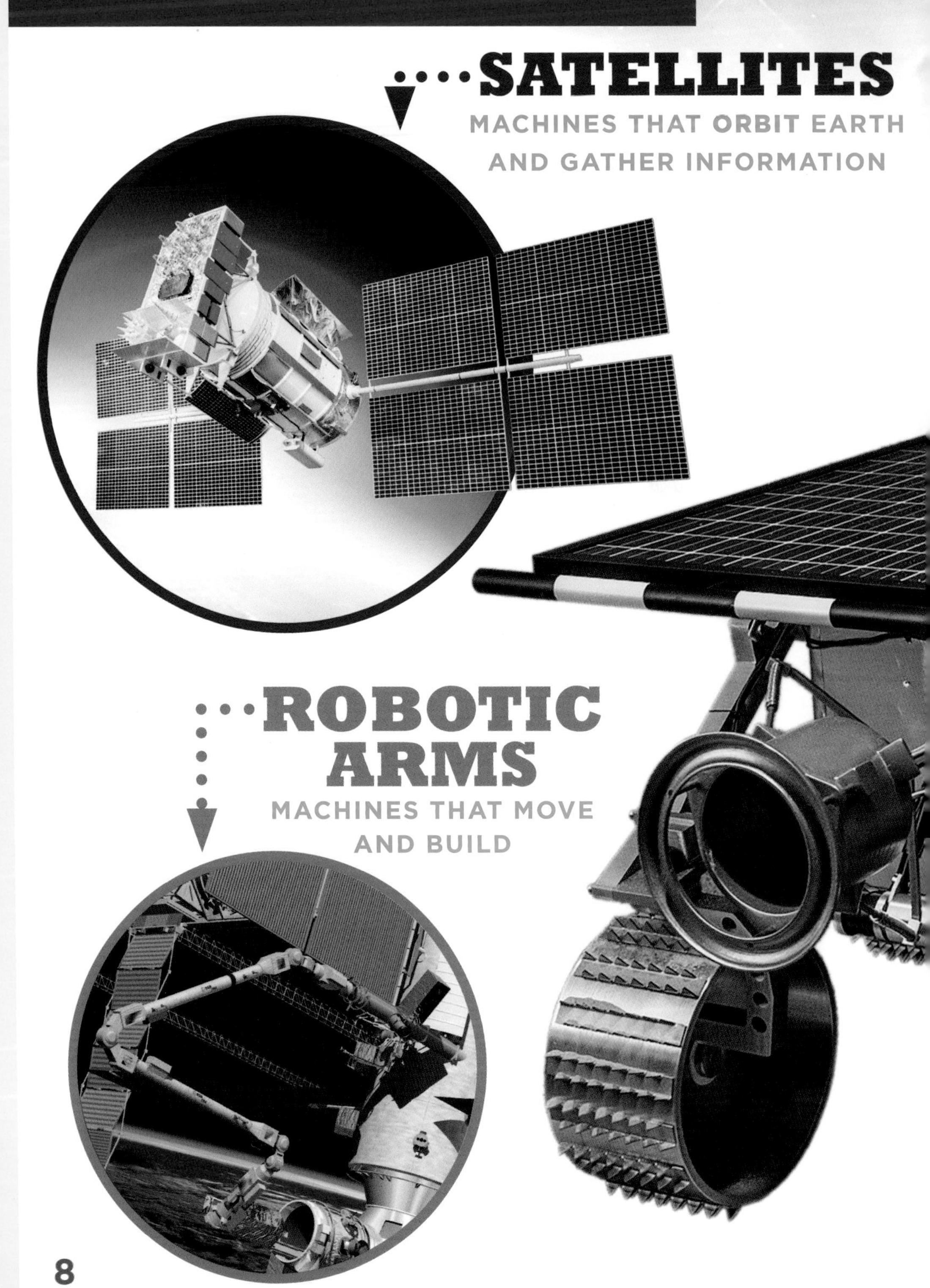

SATELLITES

MACHINES THAT **ORBIT** EARTH AND GATHER INFORMATION

ROBOTIC ARMS

MACHINES THAT MOVE AND BUILD

PROBES
SPACECRAFT THAT EXPLORE AND RESEARCH
ROVERS
VEHICLES THAT EXPLORE PLANETS AND OTHER BODIES IN SPACE

CHAPTER 2

Helping ASTRONAUTS

Robotic arms help astronauts during **missions**. Since 2001, Canadarm2 has worked at the **International Space Station** (ISS). In fact, the arm helped build parts of the station. The arm moves heavy loads. It carries astronauts too. The arm is controlled from inside the station. People on Earth can also control it.

Canadarm2 is
58 feet (18 meters) long.

Robotic Handyman

Sometimes the ISS needs repairs. That's when Dextre comes in. Dextre is a robot with arms. Power tools are attached to the arms. The bot then makes repairs. Canadarm2 can move the bot into place. It brings Dextre tools too. People on the ground control Dextre.

Dextre does jobs that astronauts used to do. That means astronauts take fewer dangerous space walks. They have more time for research too.

CHAPTER 3

Besides the moon, humans haven't visited land in space. Only bots have gone to other planets.

Since 2012, the rover Curiosity has explored Mars. Curiosity tests for signs of life. It drills, brushes, and scoops to get samples. Built-in tools run tests. The rover sends results, along with pictures, to Earth.

Curiosity isn't breaking any speed records. Its average speed is only 98 feet (30 m) per hour.

Curiosity

By the Numbers

6
number of wheels

17
NUMBER OF CAMERAS

1,982 POUNDS

(899 kilograms)

weight

10 feet

(3 m)

length

7

feet

(2 m)

height

Swarmies

Someday, small bots might replace large rovers. People are working on bots called swarmies. Compared to rovers like Curiosity, they're small, simple, and cheap.

When swarmies find something, they send out radio signals. The other bots get the signals. They rush over to help.

Many swarmies would explore a planet at once. Together, they would gather material for research. For now, these bots are still in the testing stage.

Asteroid Explorers

Scientists want to explore **comets** and **asteroids**. But these objects have very little **gravity**. A large rover would flip over if it tried to move on them.

Scientists are working on a new bot. It is called the Hedgehog. Instead of traveling on wheels, it'll hop and roll. Built-in spikes will keep its body safe when it moves. The spikes could have sensors too.

Weight of Space Robots

CURIOSITY

HEDGEHOG

SWARMIE

pounds

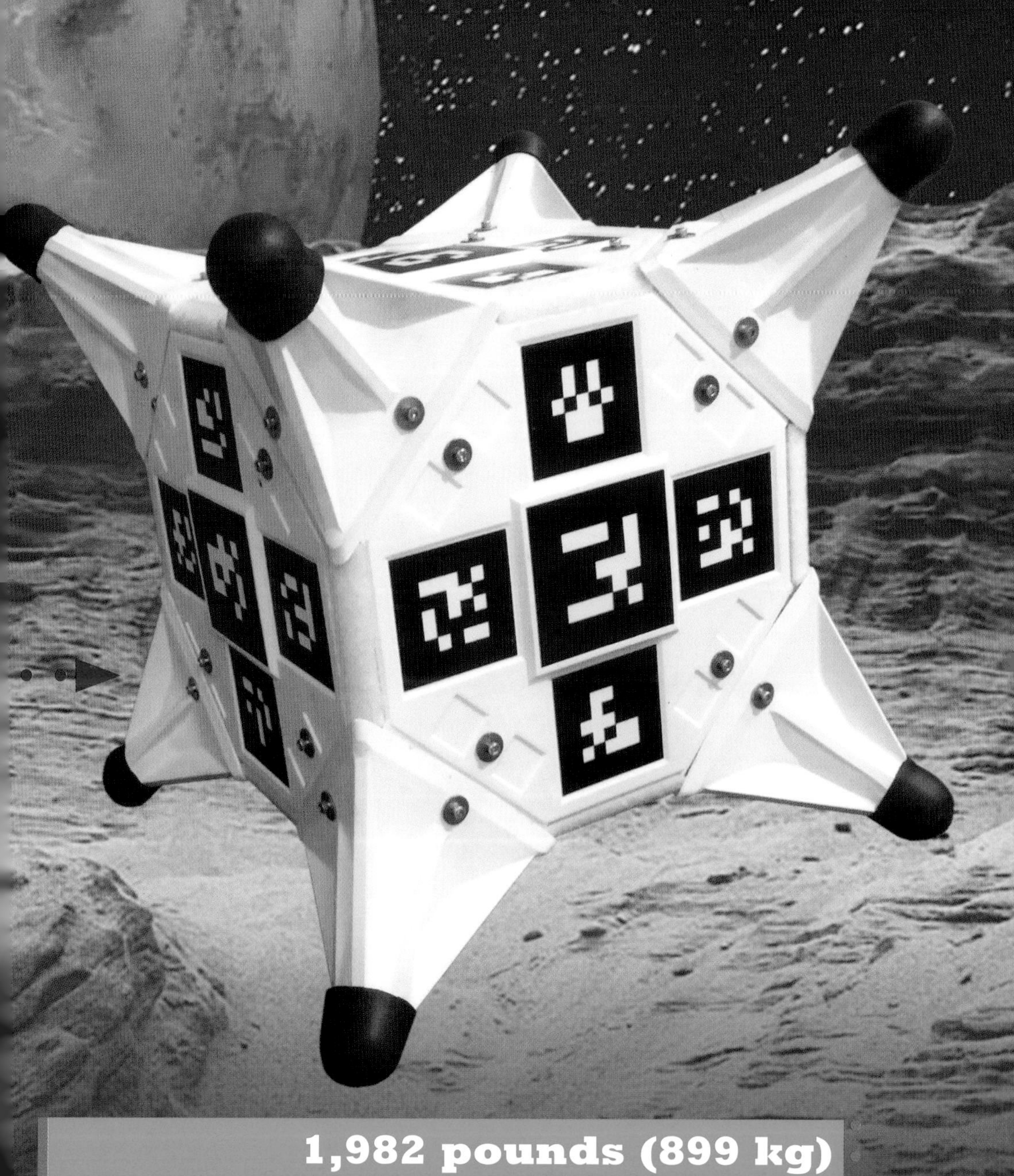

1,982 pounds (899 kg)

22 pounds (10 kg)

less than 10 pounds (4.5 kg)

0 400 800 1,200 1,600 2,000

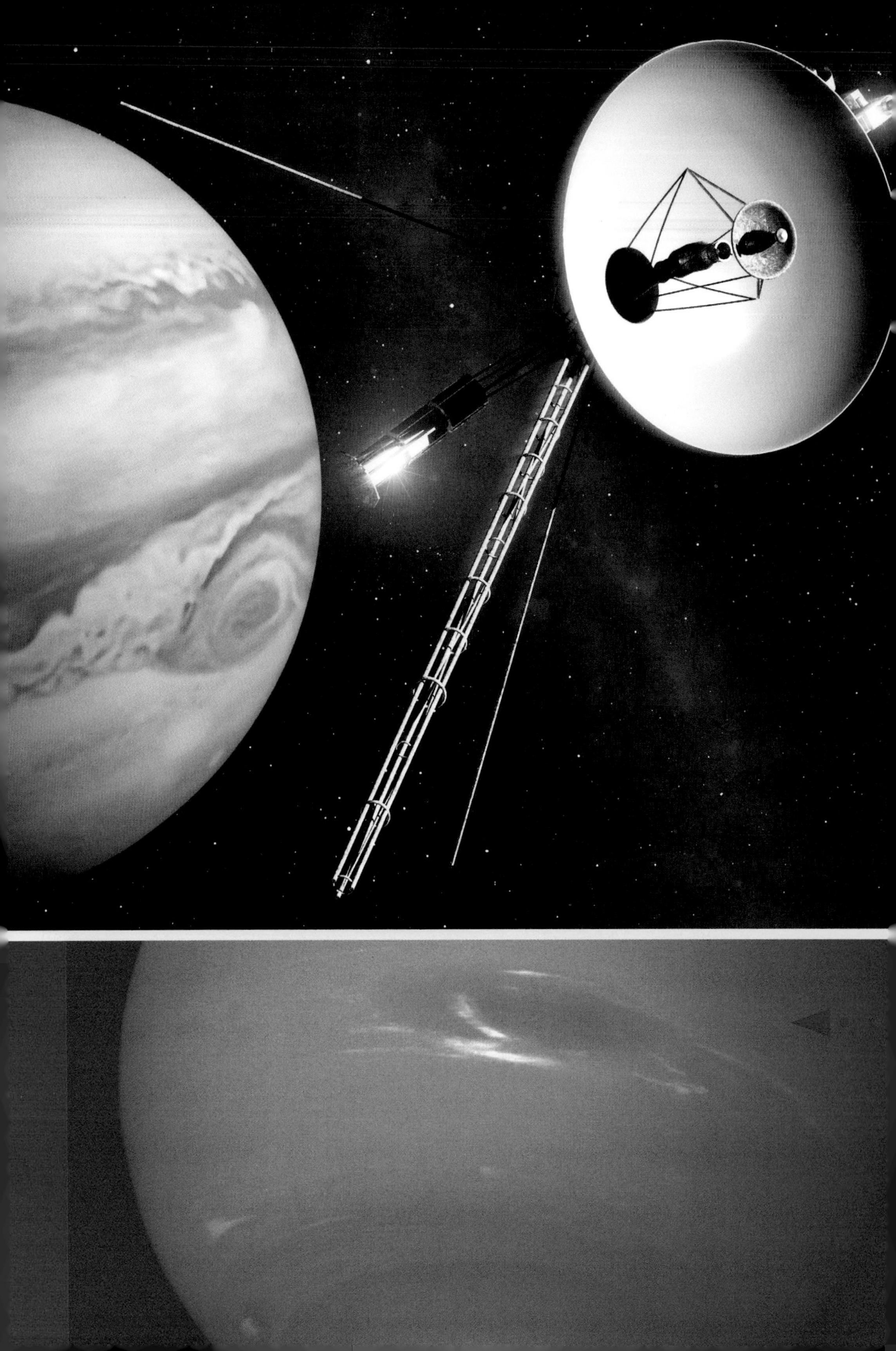

CHAPTER 4

BEYOND Our Universe?

Bots aren't new to space. In fact, two probes have been in space for 40 years.

In 1977, NASA sent two probes into space. They were Voyager 1 and 2. They have traveled farther from Earth than anything else. And they are still sending signals today!

The last Voyager pictures were taken in 1990. The cameras were shut off to save power and memory.

FAR FROM HOME

These bots are a long way from Earth!

CANADARM2
about 220 miles
(354 kilometers)

EARTH

DEXTRE
about 220 miles
(354 km)

CURIOSITY
about 140 million miles
(225 million km)

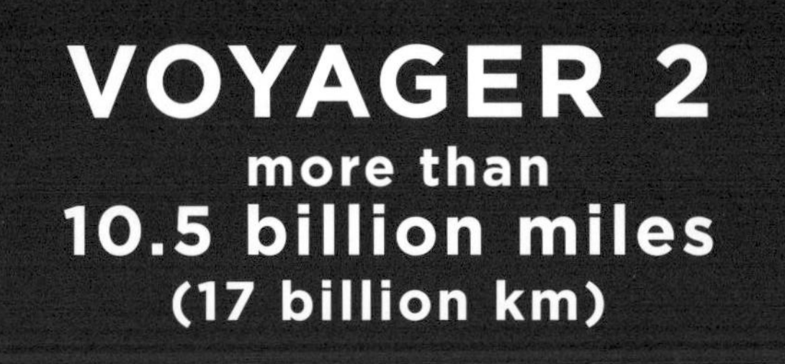

VOYAGER 1

more than
12.4 billion miles
(20 billion km)

distances will change based on the movement of the planets and ISS

Edge of Our Solar System

In 2006, NASA launched New Horizons. Its mission was to fly past Pluto. The probe reached Pluto in 2015. It took pictures of the **dwarf planet** and its moons.

At its farthest, Pluto is 4.67 billion miles (7.5 billion km) from Earth. Sending back all of the information gathered took more than a year.

Cost of Missions to Space

Mission	Cost by Millions
New Horizons	$700 MILLION
Voyagers	$865 MILLION
Curiosity	ABOUT $2,500 MILLION

COST BY MILLIONS

$0 · $300 · $600 · $900 · $1,200 · $1,500 · $1,800 · $2,100 · $2,400

To the Stars and Beyond

Research has told people a lot about space. But there is still much more to discover. People can't help but wonder what's out there. Robots will help them find out!

asteroid (AS-tuh-royd)—a large space rock that moves around the sun

comet (KOM-it)—an object in outer space that develops a long, bright tail when it passes near the sun

dwarf planet (DWAWRF PLAN-it)—a space object that orbits the sun and has a round shape but is not large enough to disturb other objects from its orbit

gravity (GRAV-i-tee)—the natural force that tends to cause physical things to move toward each other

International Space Station (in-ter-NASH-uh-nl SPEYS STEY-shun)—an orbiting spacecraft made with the cooperation of 16 nations and that is used for scientific research

mission (MISH-uhn)—a task or job that someone is given to do

orbit (AWR-bit)—the path taken by one body circling around another body

Soviet Union (SOH-ve-uht YOON-yun)—a former country in eastern Europe and northern Asia

space walk (SPEYS WAWK)—a period of activity spent outside a spacecraft by an astronaut in space

BOOKS

Furstinger, Nancy. *Robots in Space*. Robots Everywhere! Minneapolis: Lerner Publications Company, 2015.

Nagelhout, Ryan. *Space Robots.* Robots and Robotics. New York: PowerKids Press, 2017.

Spilsbury, Richard, and Louise Spilsbury. *Robots in Space.* Amazing Robots. New York: Gareth Stevens Publishing, 2016.

WEBSITES

Robotics
kidsahead.com/subjects/1-robotics

Robotics: Facts
idahoptv.org/sciencetrek/topics/robots/facts.cfm

Robots for Kids
www.sciencekids.co.nz/robots.html

INDEX